Play Ball!

By Ann Ingalls
Illustrated by Brian Martin

Reggie and Rex
have short legs.

They like to play ball.

Uh oh! They lose their ball.

They look upstairs
and downstairs.

The ball is gone.

Uh oh! They see a tall dog.

Remi likes the ball.
She chases the ball.

She cannot get the ball.

Reggie and Rex
can help!

Rex says, "Let's all play!"
And they do.

Publishing Credits

Rachelle Cracchiolo, M.S.Ed., *Publisher*
Conni Medina, M.A.Ed., *Editor in Chief*
Nika Fabienke, Ed.D., *Content Director*
Véronique Bos, *Creative Director*
Shaun Bernadou, *Art Director*
Stephanie Loureiro, *Associate Editor*
Jess Johnson, *Graphic Designer*

Image Credits: Illustrations by Brian Martin.

Library of Congress Cataloging-in-Publication Data

Names: Ingalls, Ann, author. | Martin, Brian (Brian Michael), 1978- illustrator.
Title: Play ball! / by Ann Ingalls ; illustrated by Brian Martin.
Description: Huntington Beach, CA : Teacher Created Materials, 2019. | Summary: "Meet Reggie and Rex. They like to play ball. What happens when they lose their ball?"-- Provided by publisher.
Identifiers: LCCN 2019014347 | ISBN 9781644913116 (pbk.)
Subjects: | CYAC: Balls (Sporting goods)--Fiction.
Classification: LCC PZ7.I45 Pl 2019 | DDC [E]--dc23 LC record available at https://lccn.loc.gov/2019014347

TCM Teacher Created Materials
5301 Oceanus Drive
Huntington Beach, CA 92649-1030
www.tcmpub.com

ISBN 978-1-6449-1311-6

Printed by: 590835
Printed in: China